McIlvaine's Star

McIlvaine's Star

August Derleth

ÆGYPAN PRESS

This story first appeared in *If Worlds of Science Fiction,* July, 1952.

August Derleth lived from 1909 until 1971.

Special thanks to Greg Weeks, Stephen Blundell, and the Online Distributed Proofreading Team (which can be found at http://www.pgdp.net).

McIlvaine's Star
A publication of
Ægypan Press

www.aegypan.com

Old Thaddeus McIlvaine discovered a dark star and took it for his own. Thus he inherited a dark destiny — or did he?

"Call them what you like," said Tex Harrigan. "Lost people or strayed, crackpots or warped geniuses — I know enough of them to fill an entire department of queer people. I've been a reporter long enough to have run into quite a few of them."

"For example?" I said, recognizing Harrigan's mellowness.

"Take Thaddeus McIlvaine," said Harrigan.

"I never heard of him."

"I suppose not," said Harrigan. "But I knew him. He was an eccentric old fellow who had a modest income — enough to keep up his hobbies, which were three: he played cards and chess at a tavern called Bixby's on North Clark Street; he was an amateur astronomer;

and he had the fixed idea that there was life somewhere outside this planet and that it was possible to communicate with other beings — but unlike most others, he tried it constantly with the queer machinery he had rigged up.

"Well, now, this old fellow had a trio of cronies with whom he played on occasion down at Bixby's. He had no one else to confide in. He kept them up with his progress among the stars and his communication with other life in the cosmos beyond our own, and they made a great joke out of it, from all I could gather. I suppose, because he had no one else to talk to, McIlvaine took it without complaint. Well, as I said, I never heard of him until one morning the city editor — it was old Bill Henderson then — called me in and said, 'Harrigan, we just got a lead on a fellow named Thaddeus McIlvaine who claims to have discovered a new star. Amateur astronomer up North Clark. Find him and get a story.' So I set out to track him down. . . ."

It was a great moment for Thaddeus McIlvaine. He sat down among his friends almost portentously, adjusted his spectacles, and peered over them in his usual manner, halfway between a querulous oldster and a reproachful schoolmaster.

"I've done it," he said quietly.

"Aye, and what?" asked Alexander testily.

"I discovered a new star."

"Oh," said Leopold flatly. "A cinder in your eye."

"It lies just off Arcturus," McIlvaine went on, "and it would appear to be coming closer."

"Give it my love," said Richardson with a wry smile. "Have you named it yet? Or don't the discoverers of new stars name them anymore? McIlvaine's Star — that's a good name for it. Hard a port of Arcturus, with special displays on windy nights."

McIlvaine only smiled. "It's a dark star," he said presently. "It doesn't have light." He spoke almost apologetically, as if somehow he had disappointed his friends. "I'm going to try and communicate with it."

"That's the ticket," said Alexander.

"Cut for deal," said Leopold.

That was how the news about McIlvaine's Star was received by his cronies. Afterward, after McIlvaine had dutifully played several games of euchre, Richardson conceived the idea of telephoning the *Globe* to announce McIlvaine's discovery.

"The old fellow took himself seriously," Harrigan went on. "And yet he was so damned mousy about it. I mean, you got the impression that he had been trying for so long that now he hardly believed in his star himself any longer. But there it was. He had a long, detailed story of its discovery, which was an accident, as those things usually are. They happen all the time, and his story sounded convincing enough. Just the same, you didn't feel that he really had anything. I took down notes, of course; that was routine. I got a picture of the old man, with never an idea we'd be using it.

"To tell the truth, I carried my notes around with me for a day or so before it occurred to me that it wouldn't do any harm to put a call in to Yerkes Observatory up in Wisconsin. So I did, and they confirmed McIlvaine's Star. The *Globe* had the story, did it up in fine style.

"It was two weeks before we heard from McIlvaine again. . . ."

That night McIlvaine was more than usually diffident. He was not like a man bearing a message of considerable importance to himself. He slipped into Bixby's, got a glass of beer, and approached the table where his friends sat, almost with trepidation.

"It's a nice evening for May," he said quietly.

Richardson grunted.

Leopold said, "By the way, Mac, whatever became of that star of yours? The one the papers wrote up."

"I think," said McIlvaine cautiously, "I'm quite sure — I have got in touch with them. Only," his brow wrinkled and furrowed, "I can't understand their language."

"Ah," said Richardson with an edge to his voice, "the thing for you to do is to tell them that's your star, and they'll have to speak English from now on, so you can understand them. Why, next thing we know, you'll be getting yourself a rocket or a space-ship and going over to that star to set yourself up as king or something."

"King Thaddeus the First," said Alexander loftily. "All you star-dwellers may kiss the royal foot."

"That would be unsanitary, I think," said McIlvaine, frowning.

Poor McIlvaine! They made him the butt of their jests for over an hour before he took himself off to his quarters, where he sat himself down before his telescope and found his star once more, almost huge enough to blot out Arcturus, but not quite, since it was moving away from that amber star now.

McIlvaine's star was certainly much closer to the Earth than it had been.

He tried once again to contact it with his home-made radio, and once again he received a succession of strange, rhythmic noises which he could not doubt were speech of some kind or other — a rasping, grating speech, to be sure, utterly unlike the speech of McIlvaine's own kind. It rose and fell, became impatient, urgent, despairing — McIlvaine sensed all this and strove mightily to understand.

He sat there for perhaps two hours when he received the distant impression that someone was talking to him in his own language. But there was no longer any sound on the radio. He could not understand what had taken place, but in a few moments he received the clear conviction that the inhabitants of his star had managed to discover the basic elements of his language by the simple process of reading his mind, and were now prepared to talk with him.

What manner of creatures inhabited Earth? they wished to know.

McIlvaine told them. He visualized one of his own kind and tried to put him into words. It was difficult, since he could not rid himself of the conviction that his interlocutors might be utterly alien.

They had no conception of man and doubted man's existence on any other star. There were plant-people on Venus, ant-people on Andromeda, six-legged and four-armed beings which were equal parts mineral and vegetable on Betelguese — but nothing resembling man. "You are evidently alone of your kind in the cosmos," said his interstellar correspondent.

"And what about you?" cried McIlvaine with unaccustomed heat.

Silence was his only answer, but presently he conceived a mental image which was remarkable for its vividness. But the image was of nothing he had ever seen before — of thousands upon thousands of miniature beings, utterly alien to man; they resembled amphibious insects, with thin, elongated heads, large eyes, and antennae set upon a scaled, four-legged body, with rudimentary beetlelike wings. Curiously, they seemed ageless; he could detect no difference among them — all appeared to be the same age.

"We are not, but we rejuvenate regularly," said the creature with whom he corresponded in this strange manner.

Did they have names? McIlvaine wondered.

"I am Guru," said the star's inhabitant. "You are McIlvaine."

And the civilization of their star?

Instantly he saw in his mind's eye vast cities, which rose from beneath a surface which appeared to bear no vegetation recognizable to any human eye, in a terrain which seemed to be desert, of monolithic buildings, which were windowless and had openings only of sufficient size to permit the free passage of its dwarfed dwellers. Within the buildings was evidence of a great and old civilization. . . .

"You see, McIlvaine really believed all this. What an imagination the man had! Of course, the boys at Bixby's gave him a bad time; I don't know how he stood it, but he did. And he always came back. Richardson called the story in; he took a special delight in deviling McIlvaine, and I was sent out to see the old fellow again.

"You couldn't doubt his sincerity. And yet he didn't sound touched."

"But, of course, that part about the insectlike dwellers of the star comes straight out of Wells, doesn't it?" I put in.

"Wells and scores of others," agreed Harrigan. "Wells was probably the first writer to suggest insectivorous inhabitants on Mars; his were considerably larger, though."

"Go on."

"Well, I talked with McIlvaine for quite a while. He told me all about their civilization and about his friend, Guru. You might have thought he was talking about a neighbor of his I had only to step outside to meet.

"Later on, I dropped around at Bixby's and had a talk with the boys there. Richardson let me in on a secret. He had decided to rig up a connection to McIlvaine's machine and do a little talking to the old fellow, making him believe Guru was coming through in English. He meant to give McIlvaine a harder time than ever, and once he had him believing everything he planned to say, they would wait for him at Bixby's and let him make a fool of himself.

"It didn't work out quite that way, however. . . ."

"McIlvaine, can you hear me?"

McIlvaine started with astonishment. His mental impression of Guru became confused; the voice speaking English came clear as a bell, as if from no distance at all.

"Yes," he said hesitantly.

"Well, then, listen to me, listen to Guru. We have now had enough information from you to suit our ends. Within twenty-four hours, we, the inhabitants of Ahli, will begin a war of extermination against Earth. . . ."

"But, why?" cried McIlvaine, astounded.

The image before his mind's eye cleared. The cold, precise features of Guru betrayed anger.

"There is interference," the thought-image informed him. "Leave the machine for a few moments, while we use the disintegrators."

Before he left the machine, McIlvaine had the impression of a greater machine being attached to the means of communication which the inhabitants of his star were using to communicate with him.

"McIlvaine's story was that a few moments later there was a blinding flash just outside his window," continued Harrigan. "There was also a run of instantaneous fire from the window to his machine. When he had collected his wits sufficiently, he ran outside to look. There was nothing there but a kind of greyish dust in a little mound — as if, as he put it, 'somebody had cleaned out a vacuum bag'. He went back in and examined the space from the window to the machine; there were two thin lines of dust there, hardly perceptible, just as if something had been attached to the machine and led outside.

"Now the obvious supposition is naturally that it was Richardson out there, and that the lines of dust from the window to the machine represented the wires he had attached to his microphone while McIlvaine was at Bixby's entertaining his other two cronies, but this is fact, not fiction, and the point of the episode is that Richardson disappeared from that night on."

"You investigated, of course?" I asked.

Harrigan nodded. "Quite a lot of us investigated. The police might have done better. There was a gang war on in Chicago just at that time, and Richardson was nobody with any connections. His nearest relatives weren't anxious about anything but what they might inherit; to tell the truth, his cronies at Bixby's were the only people who worried about him. McIlvaine as much as the rest of them.

"Oh, they gave the old man a hard time, all right. They went through his house with a fine-toothed comb. They dug up his yard, his cellar, and generally put him through it, figuring he was a natural to hang a murder rap on. But there was just nothing to be found, and they couldn't manufacture evidence when there was nothing to show that McIlvaine ever knew that Richardson planned to have a little fun with him.

"And no one had seen Richardson there. There was nothing but McIlvaine's word that he had heard what he said he heard. He needn't have volunteered that, but he did. After the police had finished with him, they wrote him off as a harmless nut. But the question of what happened to Richardson wasn't solved from that day to this."

"People have been known to walk out of their lives," I said. "And never come back."

"Oh, sometimes they do. Richardson didn't. Besides, if he walked out of his life here, he did so without more than the clothing he had on. So much was missing from his effects, nothing more."

"And McIlvaine?"

Harrigan smiled thinly. "He carried on. You couldn't expect him to do anything less. After all, he had worked most of his life trying to communicate with the worlds outside, and he had no intention of resigning his contact, no matter how much Richardson's disappearance upset him. For a while he believed that Guru had actually disintegrated Richardson; he offered that explanation, but by that time the dust had vanished, and he was laughed out of face. So he went back to the machine and Guru and the little excursions to Bixby's. . . ."

"What's the latest word from that star of yours?" asked Leopold, when McIlvaine came in.

"They want to rejuvenate me," said McIlvaine, with a certain shy pleasure.

"What's that?" asked Alexander sourly.

"They say they can make me young again. Like them up there. They never die. They just live so long, and then they rejuvenate, they begin all over. It's some kind of a process they have."

"And I suppose they're planning to come down and fetch you up there and give you the works, is that it?" asked Alexander.

"Well, no," answered McIlvaine. "Guru says there's no need for that — it can be done through the machine; they can work it like the disintegrators; it puts you back to thirty or twenty or wherever you like."

"Well, I'd like to be twenty-five myself again," admitted Leopold.

"I'll tell you what, Mac," said Alexander. "You go ahead and try it; then come back and let us know how it works. If it does, we'll all sit in."

"Better make your will first, though, just in case."

"Oh, I did. This afternoon."

Leopold choked back a snicker. "Don't take this thing too seriously, Mac. After all, we're short one of us now. We'd hate to lose you, too."

McIlvaine was touched. "Oh, I wouldn't change," he hastened to assure his friends. "I'd just be younger, that's all. They'll just work on me through the machine, and overnight I'll be rejuvenated."

"That's certainly a little trick that's got it all over monkey glands," conceded Alexander, grinning.

"Those little bugs on that star of yours have made scientific progress, I'd say," said Leopold.

"They're not bugs," said McIlvaine with faint indignation. "They're people, maybe not just like you and me, but they're people just the same."

He went home that night filled with anticipation. He had done just what he had promised himself he would do, arranging everything for his rejuvenation. Guru had been astonished to learn that people on Earth simply died when there was no necessity of doing so; he had made the offer to rejuvenate McIlvaine himself.

McIlvaine sat down to his machine and turned the complex knobs until he was en rapport with his dark star. He waited for a long time, it seemed, before he knew his contact had been closed. Guru came through.

"Are you ready, McIlvaine?" he asked soundlessly.

"Yes. All ready," said McIlvaine, trembling with eagerness.

"Don't be alarmed now. It will take several hours," said Guru.

"I'm not alarmed," answered McIlvaine.

And indeed he was not; he was filled with an exhilaration akin to mysticism, and he sat waiting for what he was certain must be the experience above all others in his prosaic existence.

"McIlvaine's disappearance coming so close on Richardson's gave us a beautiful story," said Harrigan. "The only trouble was, it wasn't new when the *Globe* got around to it. We had lost our informant in Richardson; it never occurred to Alexander or Leopold to telephone us or anyone about McIlvaine's unaccountable absence from Bixby's. Finally, Leopold went over to McIlvaine's house to find out whether the old fellow was sick.

"A young fellow opened up.

"'Where's McIlvaine?' Leopold asked.

"'I'm McIlvaine,' the young fellow answered.

"'Thaddeus McIlvaine,' Leopold explained.

"'That's my name,' was the only answer he got.

"'I mean the Thaddeus McIlvaine who used to play cards with us over at Bixby's,' said Leopold.

"He shook his head. 'Sorry, you must be looking for someone else.'

"'What're you doing here?' Leopold asked then.

"'Why, I inherited what my uncle left,' said the young fellow.

"And, sure enough, when Leopold talked to me and persuaded me to go around with him to McIlvaine's lawyer, we found that the old fellow had made a will and left everything to his nephew, a namesake. The stipulations were clear enough; among them was the express wish that if anything happened to him, the elder Thaddeus McIlvaine, of no matter what nature, but particularly something allowing a reasonable doubt of his death, the nephew was still to be permitted to take immediate possession of the property and effects."

"Of course, you called on the nephew," I said.

Harrigan nodded. "Sure. That was the indicated course, in any event. It was routine for both the press and the police. There was nothing suspicious about his story; it was straightforward enough, except for one or two little details. He never did give us any precise address; he just mentioned Detroit once. I called up a friend on one of the papers there and put him up to looking up Thaddeus McIlvaine; the only young man of that name he could find appeared to be the same man as the present inhabitant's uncle, though the description fit pretty well."

"There was a resemblance, then?"

"Oh, sure. One could have imagined that old Thaddeus McIlvaine had looked somewhat like his nephew when he himself was a young man. But don't let the old man's rigmarole about rejuvenation make too deep an impression on you. The first thing the young fellow did was to get rid of that machine of his uncle's.

Can you imagine his uncle having done something like that?"

I shook my head, but I could not help thinking what an ironic thing it would have been if there had been something to McIlvaine's story, and in the process to which he had been subjected from out of space he had not been rejuvenated so much as just sent back in time, in which case he would have no memory of the machine nor of the use to which it had been put. It would have been as ironic for the inhabitants of McIlvaine's star, too; they would doubtless have looked forward to keeping this contact with Earth open and failed to realize that McIlvaine's construction differed appreciably from theirs.

"He virtually junked it. Said he had no idea what it could be used for, and didn't know how to operate it."

"And the telescope?"

"Oh, he kept that. He said he had some interest in astronomy and meant to develop that if time permitted."

"So much ran in the family, then."

"Yes. More than that. Old McIlvaine had a trick of seeming shy and self-conscious. So did this nephew of his. Wherever he came from, his origins must have been backward. I suspect that he was ashamed of them, and if I had to guess, I'd put him in the Kentucky hill-country or the Ozarks. Modern concepts seemed to be pretty well too much for him, and his thinking would have been considerably more natural at the turn of the century.

"I had to see him several times. The police chivvied him a little, but not much; he was so obviously innocent of everything that there was nothing for them in him. And the search for the old man didn't last long; no one had seen him after that last night at Bixby's, and, since everyone had already long since concluded that he was mentally a little off center, it was easy to conclude that he had wandered away somewhere, probably an amnesiac. That he might have anticipated that is indicated in the hasty preparation of his will, which came out of the blue, said Barnevall, who drew it up for him.

"I felt sorry for him."

"For whom?"

"The nephew. He seemed so lost, you know — like a man who wanted to remember something, but couldn't. I noticed that several times when I tried to talk to him; I had the feeling each time that there was something he wanted desperately to say, it hovered always on the rim of his awareness, but somehow there was no bridge to it, no clue to put it into words. He tried so hard for something he couldn't put his finger on."

"What became of him?"

"Oh, he's still around. I think he found a job somewhere. As a matter of fact, I saw him just the other evening. He had apparently just come from work and he was standing in front of Bixby's with his face pressed to the window looking in. I came up nearby and watched him. Leopold and Alexander were sitting inside — a couple of lonely old men looking out. And a lonely young man looking in. There was something in McIlvaine's face — that same thing I had noticed so often before, a kind of expression that seemed to say there was something he ought to know, something he ought to remember, to do, to say, but there was no way in which he could reach back to it."

"Or forward," I said with a wry smile.

"As you like," said Harrigan. "Pour me another, will you?"

I did and he took it.

"That poor devil!" he muttered. "He'd be happier if he could only go back where he came from."

"Wouldn't we all?" I asked. "But nobody ever goes home again. Perhaps McIlvaine never had a home like that."

"You'd have thought so if you could have seen his face looking in at Leopold and Alexander. Oh, it may have been a trick of the streetlight there, it may have been my imagination. But it sticks to my memory, and I keep thinking how alike the two were — old McIlvaine trying so desperately to find someone who could believe him, and his nephew now trying just as hard to find someone to accept him or a place he could accept on the only terms he knows."

THE END

www.ingramcontent.com/pod-product-compliance
Lightning Source LLC
Chambersburg PA
CBHW030416310726
48979CB00002B/435

9781463896720